When Jo Louis Won the Title

Belinda Rochelle   Illustrated by Larry Johnson

Houghton Mifflin Company   Boston

To my nephews, Lance, Maurice and Tim
To my daughter, Shevon
And to my friend, Deborah

— B.R.

To my Grandchildren, Brandon and Brooke Thorpe and to God
for giving me more wisdom and patience to enjoy them

— L.J.

Text copyright © 1994 by Belinda Rochelle
Illustrations copyright © 1994 by Larry Johnson

For information about this and other Houghton Mifflin
trade and reference books and multimedia products,
visit The Bookstore at Houghton Mifflin on the World
Wide Web at http://www.hmco.com/trade/.

Library of Congress Cataloging-in-Publication Data

Rochelle, Belinda.
    When Jo Louis won the title / by Belinda Rochelle ; illustrated by
Larry Johnson.
    p.   cm.
    Summary: Jo's grandfather helps her feel better about herself when
he tells her the story about why she is named for the heavyweight
boxing champion, Joe Louis.
    RNF ISBN 0-395-66614-7   PAP ISBN 0-395-81657-2
    [1. Afro-Americans — Fiction. 2. Names, Personal — Fiction.
3. Grandfathers — Fiction.]   I. Johnson, Larry, 1949-   ill.
II. Title.
PZ7.R5864Wh   1994   93-34317
[E] — dc20   CIP
                          AC

Printed in the United States of America

BVG   10   9   8   7   6   5   4   3

JO LOUIS sat perched on the top step of ten steps,
waiting for her grandfather, John Henry.

"Is that my favorite girl
in the whole wide world?"
he said as he strolled up the street.
He leaned over and picked up Jo Louis,
swung her round and round
until her ponytails whirled
like the propellers of a plane,
swung her round and round
until they were both dizzy with gasps,
swung her round and round
until they were both dizzy with giggles.

John Henry's brown eyes twinkled as he returned
Jo Louis to the top step and sat down next to her.
The smile quickly disappeared from Jo Louis's face.
"Why such a sad face on a pretty girl?" he asked.

Tomorrow was a special day for Jo Louis.
The first day at a new school.
"I don't want to go to school!"
Jo Louis said to her grandfather.
"I don't want to be the new girl in a
new neighborhood at a new school."

John Henry put his arm around her
and pulled her close.
"Why don't you want to go to school?" he asked.
"I'll probably be the shortest kid in class,
or I'll be the one who can't run as fast
as the other kids.
I finish every race last."
"It's just a matter of time
before a new school is an old school.
Just a matter of time
before you'll be able to run really fast,
and you won't always finish last,"
he said, patting her hand.
"What's the real reason you don't want
to go to school?" John Henry asked.

Jo Louis shook her head.
It was hard to explain.
She just knew it would happen.
Someone would ask THE question.
IT was THE question,
the same question each and every time
she met someone new:
"What's your name?"
It was that moment,
that question,
that made Jo Louis want to disappear.
And it really wouldn't make a difference
if she were taller,
and it wouldn't make a difference
that she was the new kid in school,
and it wouldn't make a difference
if she could run really fast.
She just wished that she didn't have to
tell anyone her name.

Her grandfather picked her up
and placed her on his knee.
"Let me tell you a story," he said.

"When I was just a young boy
living in Mississippi," he began,
"I used to dream about moving north.
To me it was the promised land.
I wanted to find a good job in the big city.
Cities like Chicago, St. Louis.
But everybody, I mean everybody,
talked about Harlem in New York City.
Going north, it was all anybody
ever talked about.
I would sit on the front porch and
just daydream about those big-city places.
The way some folks told it
everything was perfect.
Even the streets in the big city
were paved with gold,
and it was all there just waiting for me."
John Henry's eyes sparkled as his voice quickened.
"When I saved enough money,
I crowded onto the train
with other small-town folks headed north.
Everything I owned fit into a torn, tattered suitcase
and a brown box wrapped in string."

"I rode the train all day and all night.
Like a snake winding its way across the Mississippi River,
that train moved slowly through farmlands and flatland,
over mountains and valleys,
until it reached its final destination."

Jo Louis closed her eyes.
She loved her grandfather's stories—
his words were like wings and other things.
She listened closely until she felt
she was right there with him.

"'New York City! New York! New York!'
the conductor bellowed as the train pulled
into the station."

"I headed straight to Harlem.
I had never seen buildings so tall.
They almost seemed to touch the sky.
Even the moon looked different in the big city.
The moonlight was bright and shining,
the stars skipped across the sky.
The streets sparkled in the night sky's light.
It was true!
The streets did seem to be paved in gold!
I walked up and down city streets
that stretched wide and long.
I walked past a fancy nightclub,
where you could hear the moaning of a saxophone
and a woman singing so sad, so soft, and so slow
that the music made me long for home."

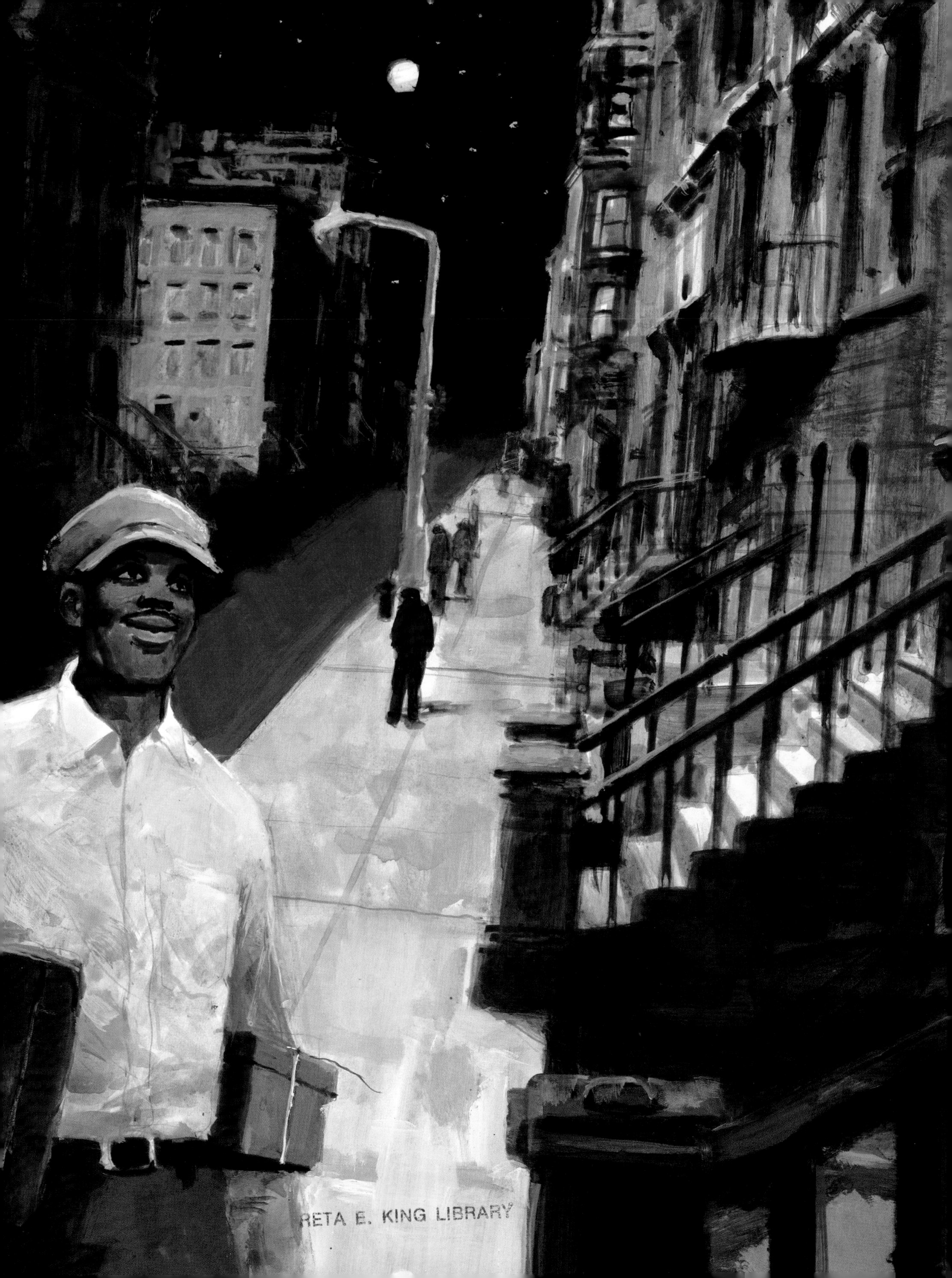

"And then, all of a sudden
the sad music changed to happy music.
That saxophone and singing started to swing.
Hundreds of people spilled out into the sidewalks,
waving flags, scarves,
waving handkerchiefs and tablecloths.
Hundreds of people filled the streets
with noise and laughter,
waving hats and anything and everything,
filling the sky with bright colors of red,
white, green, yellow, blue, purple, and orange."

"Everybody was clapping,
hands were raised high to the sky.
Up and down the street,
people were shouting and singing.
Cars were beeping their horns;
bells were ringing.
'Excuse me.' I patted a woman on the shoulder.
'What's going on?' I asked.
The woman smiled.
She was pretty with soft, brown hair
and a friendly smile.
'Why, haven't you heard?' she said,
'Joe Louis won the title fight.
My name is Mary'—she held out her hand—
'and your name is … ?'"

John Henry smiled and hugged Jo Louis close.
"It was a special night for me.
It was a special night for black people everywhere.
Joe Louis was the greatest boxer in the world.
He was a hero.
That night he won the fight of his life.
A fight that a lot of people thought he would lose.
Some folks said he was too slow,
others said he wasn't strong enough.
But he worked hard and won.
It was a special night,
my first night in the big city,
and Joe Louis won the fight.
But the night was special for another reason."

"It was the night you met Grandma," Jo Louis said,
and she started to smile.
"It was a special night that I'll never forget.
I named your father Joe Louis,
and he named you, his first child, Jo Louis, too."
Her grandfather tickled her nose.
"That was the night you won the title.
You should be very proud of your name.
Every name has a special story."

The next day Jo Louis took a deep breath
as she walked into her new school classroom
and slipped into a seat.
The boy sitting next to Jo Louis tapped her on the shoulder.
"My name is Lester. What's your name?"
Jo answered slowly, "My name is Jo . . . Jo Louis."
She balled her fist
and closed her eyes
and braced herself.
She waited,
waited for the laughter,
waited for the jokes.
She peeked out of one eye,
then she peeked out the other eye.

"Wow, what a great name!" he said, and smiled.